OLD MIND, YOUNG BODY (Body Switch)

By Lance Majestik

OLD MIND, YOUNG BODY (Body Switch)

PAPERBACK ISBN: 978-1-989683-16-3

TABLE OF CONTENTS

CHAPTER 1 (Alone and Unappreciated)

Old age sucked.

In April I retired from the practice of law two weeks after the governor of New York shut down the state economy in an effort to stop the spread of the Covid-19 virus.

The shutdown was supposed to last for two weeks but just before that period expired, Cuomo extended the shutdown for another month.

Despite my advancing age, my intellect was still sharp. The authorities wouldn't give up their new-found power to screw with our lives until public sentiment compelled them to do so.

In March and April the media and the medical community had terrified folks that this virus was some sort of deadly plague which might soon wipe us all out.

I suspected that shutdowns and other restrictions on our basic freedoms would be with us for a long, long time.

I opted to retire rather than work under such onerous conditions.

It was quite painless to close up my law practice. My office landlord was looking to expand his legal office and we came to an agreement with a minimum of negotiation.

Richard took over my handful of existing files and agreed to store my closed-out files.

For the past couple of years I had been whittling down my business in preparation for quitting practice. I had been an attorney in the small city of Ogdensburg, New York since I was called to the state legal bar in March of 1973.

Forty-seven years was more than enough time to call it the end of my career.

By the middle of April I was a man of leisure even though the shutdowns meant that there was nowhere to go.

I guess I should introduce myself.

My name is Peter Montrose and I'm a widower with no kids and not much of a life.

My wife Deidre died in 1999 and I've lived alone ever since.

My legal practice has been the bulwark of my life since Deidre passed away.

For a number of years I played a lot of duplicate bridge as an enjoyable hobby but my regular partner died two years ago and I gave up the game.

Another impediment to my mobility occurred a year ago when two things happened almost simultaneously.

My 2002 Chevrolet Cavalier finally died on me. I had owned the little beast since I purchased it brand new in February of that year.

A week later I was at my eye doctor's office for a check-up and learned that my eyesight had deteriorated significantly since my last visit.

The damage couldn't be repaired and the optometrist was forced to notify the Department of Motor Vehicles about my condition. They yanked my driver's license which severely curtailed my ability to get around town.

Fortunately my small apartment was within relatively easy walking distance of my legal office so I continued working until this past April.

My seventy-third birthday came and went on July 26th and I celebrated the event alone in my apartment with a six-pack of beer.

Old age was strange. My eyesight and physical stamina were shot but my hearing and sense of smell were still excellent. Being able to hear well was an asset but having an acute sense of smell was a definite impediment. I was regularly bombarded with appalling odors which most folks couldn't even detect.

It was a curse being able to detect foul odors but I'd learned to live with it.

The morning following my beer-filled birthday greeted me with a nasty hangover and a burning desire to get out of Ogdensburg permanently.

I gave my landlord notice to vacate my apartment on August 31st and used that month to sort out my affairs and decide what to do with the bit of time I had left on this lonely planet.

I cashed in all my investments and transferred the proceeds into my bank checking account. I had no further need to increase my net worth.

By the 26th of August I had set my itinerary.

Peter Montrose was going to travel around America despite the Covid-19 restrictions.

Like Jack Reacher, my home would be whatever motel room I happened to occupy on any given night.

I packed a sports bag with a few clothes, my electric razor, toothbrush, one set of cutlery, my passport plus a notebook and pen with which to record my adventures.

My wallet was stuffed with cash and I could use my bank card to obtain more money wherever I happened to be. My social security payments and IRA withdrawals would continue to be automatically deposited into my bank account each month.

Because of my impaired eyesight, I no longer required eyeglasses. My ability to read was relatively intact but my distance vision would be forever impaired.

I told no one about my travel plans, mainly because no one in town gave a shit what Peter Montrose was up to.

In the back of my mind the purpose of my excursion was only slightly vague.

This adventure would allow me to finally die in peace and be reunited with Deidre assuming such a thing was even possible.

Peter Montrose was on his way to meet his Maker.

With any luck I could actually enjoy my farewell travel adventure before my time on this planet expired.

CHAPTER 2 (Travelling Oldster)

I had considered crossing the border into Canada but because of the virus, both countries had closed their borders for ordinary travelers. Only commercial vehicles were permitted to move from country to country.

Since that option was off the table, I decided to let fate guide me.

My apartment was empty. I had been sleeping on a foam cushion for the past few nights since the Goodwill truck had arrived to cart away my furniture.

On Wednesday morning I slept in until ten o'clock after which I threw the foam cushion into the dumpster behind the small apartment building.

I handed the keys in to the landlord and informed him that I was now fully vacated.

With my small sports bag in hand, I walked to the bus station and purchased a ticket on the next available bus which was a coach to Syracuse with various stops along the way.

The first portion of the trip would have been moderately scenic as we followed the St. Lawrence River southwest to Alexandria Bay where the bus made a brief stop to pick up additional passengers.

Unfortunately because of my restricted eyesight, all I saw in the distance were vague blurs.

Being forced to wear the face mask on the bus was also quite aggravating as were the foul odors. I began to wonder if any of the passengers had bothered to bathe in the past week.

The bus continued on its journey with one further stop at Watertown.

It was almost four o'clock by the time we pulled into the Syracuse bus station.

My choices now were to get a hotel room or buy another ticket to some random destination, perhaps utilizing an overnight bus in order to save the cost of a hotel room.

When I hopped off the coach, I did wander over to the departure panels to see what options were available but after examining the possibilities, I decided that I didn't want to ruin the first night of my adventure by having an uncomfortable sleep on a smelly bus.

I asked a ticket clerk if there were any hotels or motels within walking distance of the bus depot.

"There's a really old hotel two blocks west of here but it's sort of a dive. You'd need to grab a cab in order to get to any of the nicer establishments."

I thanked the woman and went outside where I began to walk in a westerly direction.

The hotel reminded me of the old hotels in Ogdensburg from my earliest days in practice, the sort inhabited by drunks who spent their days drinking draft beer in the men's tap rooms. Every single one of those old hotels had been consumed by fire over the course of the ensuing decades or simply demolished to make way for some modern building.

There was a photograph just inside the main entrance which informed me that this Quinte Hotel was constructed in 1910.

The smell of beer permeated the whole place and I couldn't even find the check-in desk.

I wandered down the hallway and found myself in the main bar area. There were a few old men scattered around at the tables and an employee standing behind a long but empty bar.

"Excuse me, sir. I'm looking to rent a room for the night. Do you have any rooms available?"

"Will it be just for the one night?"

"That's correct."

"There is one room on the top floor but the elevator doesn't work. You can have that one for $39 plus tax."

"I'll take it. Does the hotel have a restaurant?"

"No, but in this bar we do sell hot dogs and potato chips."

I paid for the room with cash, obtained my key and walked up four flights of stairs to my Room 404.

It was no delight. The ancient wallpaper was faded all over, peeling or torn off in many spots, and sported a myriad of water stains from various leaks over the decades.

The ceiling also appeared to be badly stained but my vision really couldn't be relied on for accuracy and I didn't feel like standing on a chair to make a closer inspection.

The bed felt comfortable when I laid down it. At least I should sleep well. It had been wise to get a room rather than take an overnight bus.

There was a photograph on the wall dated 1911 showing the hotel back in its glory days.

I rested for an hour and then walked down the stairs to the tap room.

Although I sat alone up at the bar and no one spoke with me, I ate two hot dogs and two servings of potato chips, washed down with three large mugs of draft beer which were cold and refreshing.

In the big mirror behind the bar, I surreptitiously observed the other patrons, every one of whom despite my impaired vision looked to be down on their luck.

Only the bartender was forced to wear a face mask.

At eight o'clock I stood up and wandered back up to my room. I was quite inebriated but felt that it had been an excellent first day of my late life travel adventure.

Before hitting the sack, I had a nice bath since there was no shower attachment.

Then I climbed into my pajamas and crawled into bed.

My thoughts darted all over the place while I waited for sleep to overtake me.

Overall my life had been quite unremarkable. I'd been exceedingly happy right up to the time when the cancer snatched Deidre from me.

The twenty-one years following her death had been sad and lonely.

Now ill health, namely rotten eyesight combined with an assortment of regular aches and pains was attempting to make the final years of my life miserable.

Other than sharing a great marriage with Deidre, I'd accomplished nothing significant during my entire life. I'd never won any landmark legal cases back when I handled litigation matters, and after I stopped taking on any court work once Deidre got sick, my legal practice had been comprised solely of real estate transactions. I even stopped doing wills and estates because I never hired any staff after Deidre died. She had been my legal secretary beginning a few months after our marriage and we had operated the office together until she got too ill to work.

It struck me that I would have been better off if I had died at the same time as my poor wife.

This travelling oldster had morphed over the years into a useless slab of miserable humanity.

I had no idea where my destination would be tomorrow. Again I'd let fate decide for me once I arrived back at the Syracuse bus station.

CHAPTER 3 (Completely Disoriented)

My head was spinning by the time I drifted off to sleep. I put the sensation down to imbibing a bit too much beer.

The next thing I knew, daylight was streaming in the window.

I opened my eyes a bit wider.

Surprisingly I didn't have a hangover. That was a bonus.

As my mind began emerging into reality, it dawned on me that I felt great. Usually my old body was a mass of morning aches and pains.

I rolled over from my right side onto my back.

That's when the first anomaly struck me. The water stains on the ceiling were no longer noticeable. I wondered if my eyesight had deteriorated during the night. Perhaps the stains were still present but they were too far away for me to distinguish them.

I glanced back to the window.

Something was different but I couldn't put my finger on exactly what had changed.

Then it hit me.

The ratty wallpaper was missing and the wall was painted off-white. That wasn't possible.

I turned my head and began to take in the rest of this room.

It wasn't my seedy Quinte Hotel room.

Somehow I had woken up in an upscale bedroom. There was an ornate old-fashioned deep rose loveseat at the opposite end of the room and the bedroom furniture all matched. The pieces looked to be quite new but had been constructed in an antique style.

I sat up.

There was deep rose wall-to-wall carpet on the floor.

Even more startling, it appeared that someone had slept beside me in the bed. The covers were pulled away on that side of the bed as if someone had just been there.

It took me a moment to realize that I was having a bizarre but incredibly realistic dream. My eyesight was perfect and I rather liked the new me in this dream.

I lay back down in an attempt to contemplate what was happening to me.

No sooner had my head rested on the pillow when the door opened and a young boy entered.

"Who are you?" I inquired.

The boy started laughing.

"Don't be stupid, Dad. Mom told me to wake you up. Breakfast is ready."

He turned around and left.

I slowly climbed out of bed and stood up.

Instead of my own pajamas, I was wearing some other man's pajama bottoms and tee-shirt.

My arms were now definitely much bigger and more muscular. They weren't the matchsticks normally attached to my seventy-three year old body.

There was a bathroom off this bedroom so I walked in only to glance in the mirror and discover that I was no longer me.

The handsome dude staring back at me wearing my own perplexed expression was a total stranger.

I raised my arms and turned around a couple of times to confirm that Peter Montrose now inhabited the body of a much younger man.

I used the toilet, washed my face and found a man's dressing gown in the walk-in closet adjacent to this bathroom.

Perhaps I'd died overnight in the Syracuse hotel room and had been reincarnated in this other guy's body.

Whatever the reason, I was a totally honest guy and had to make full disclosure to the young kid as well as his mother.

There was no better way to accomplish that goal than to be brutally frank.

I put on a pair of slippers which looked to be much too big for my feet but which turned out to fit me perfectly.

How would I manage to explain the inexplicable?

CHAPTER 4 (Full Disclosure)

I spotted the stairs as soon as I ventured out into the hallway.

Voices were emanating from downstairs so I followed the sounds and soon found myself entering the kitchen.

A very pretty but also very pregnant woman was at the stove while the young kid I had briefly met was sitting at the kitchen table.

"Good morning, honey," the woman cooed. "Did you sleep well?"

"I think I slept a bit too well. When you're finished with what you're doing, I need to speak with you and this young man."

"What has Donnie done now?" she inquired.

"It's not about anything Donnie has done. It's about me."

"Eat your breakfast first. Then we can talk. I've already eaten. I've been up since seven o'clock."

The woman's comment made me realize that I was famished. She put a plate of pancakes in front of me and I devoured them after smothering the flapjacks with margarine and syrup.

When I had finished the last of my orange juice, the woman sat down at the table.

"You have our full and complete attention, Paul. What did you want to talk about?"

"To start with I'm going to ask you a series of questions. Please answer them honestly."

"Is this a game, Dad?"

"There's a purpose to my questions. Firstly, have I suffered a head injury recently?"

"Of course you haven't, Paul. Are you having those flashbacks again from your time in Afghanistan?"

"I don't think so. What is the date right now including the year?"

Donnie answered.

"This is fun. Today is Thursday, the 27th of August, 2020."

"That's good because it correlates to my own concept of time. I'm in the present, not the past or the future. Where am I right now? By that I mean what city and country is this?"

"You're beginning to worry me, Paul. Why are you asking these strange questions?"

"I woke up completely disoriented this morning. Before we start examining that issue, I need to determine my current location as well as the time frame I'm in."

"Explain what you mean by completely disoriented. Do you recognize Donnie and me?"

"I'm afraid not but it gets even weirder than that. Where are we right now?"

"This is our home in a suburb of Washington, D.C. I'm calling our doctor."

"Humor me for a bit longer. My name is Peter Montrose. I'm a retired lawyer from Ogdensburg, New York. Yesterday I headed off on a bus trip and got a room in a dumpy old hotel in Syracuse. A few minutes ago I woke up in your bedroom occupying this rather impressive body of a much younger man. In my own life I'm seventy-three with dreadful eyesight, an unruly mop of pure white hair and a boatload of aggravating physical ailments."

The woman began to cry.

"I'm so sorry to upset you, young lady. Please compose yourself so we can make some sense out of the body switch. I've already concluded that I'm not dreaming so I'm working on the logical hypothesis that I've been put in your husband's body for a reason."

"What reason could there possibly be other than the demons from your military service have come back with a vengeance?"

"That is definitely not the answer. I have seventy-three years of intensive memories about my life and absolutely none of Paul's. I can envisage two more realistic possibilities."

"I'm listening."

"What's your name? I don't want to keep calling you young lady or miss."

"I'm Cindy Skelding."

"Is Paul's last name also Skelding?"

"Yes."

"Either I've been put in Paul's body to accomplish something important that he was incapable of handling, or he has been put in my body to prevent or do something that I was somehow unable to handle. Perhaps we've been switched in order for both of us to do something good for mankind."

"That doesn't make any sense."

"At least it's a starting point. Does Paul work?"

"Yes. Right now he's a personal aide and bodyguard to a Congresswoman from Georgia. He's off until tomorrow when Representative Carrie Brown returns to Washington from Atlanta."

"I hope you can teach me before then as much as you know about

Paul's duties. Presumably whatever entity placed me here expects me to live Paul's life until the mission is accomplished."

Donnie piped up at that point.

"I can help you. Dad took me with him for two days last month when they were having a bring-your-child-to-work event."

"Even though I'm a lawyer, I'm totally unremarkable. That makes it puzzling why I'm been shunted into Paul's body. It must relate to something that I would recognize as a danger because of my legal training but Paul wouldn't notice. Can you hazard even a wild guess as to what that might be?"

"I'm afraid not. Paul took an oath of non-disclosure and isn't allowed to tell us much about his job but he has indicated that he has very few responsibilities."

"In that case Carrie Brown will see right through me within minutes. I've never even held let alone fired a gun and know nothing about firearms or personal protection. I've just had an idea. Maybe Paul can help me."

"I don't follow you."

"Let's call the Quinte Hotel in Syracuse. I'm in Room 404. Paul might still be in my room although I didn't notice any telephone there. It was a real dump."

"I've got a better idea," Donnie piped in. "Call your smart phone instead."

"I don't own one, Donnie. I never wanted to be available at all hours of the day and night for clients to bother me. It's good to know that you're on the ball. Surely we can get through this together somehow. It doesn't make sense that Paul and I would get our bodies switched if we have no reasonable chance of accomplishing whatever we're supposed to do."

"I'll phone the hotel," Cindy responded. "I've found their phone number on my smart phone."

Cindy put her phone on speaker mode and made the call.

The reply was a bit disheartening.

The occupant of Room 404 had checked out just fifteen minutes earlier.

"Could you describe the gentleman?" I asked.

"He was an old gentleman with white hair and a limp. He had a sports bag with him and seemed very confused. He asked me when he had checked in and what name he had used to do so. I advised him that he had arrived late yesterday afternoon. I checked our registration book but the signature was unreadable. We're not very organized around here. He also asked what day it was and if this city was Ogdensburg. I informed him that he was in Syracuse."

"Did he happen to mention where he was heading?" I inquired.

"No he didn't. He did ask if the hotel had a pay phone but we don't."

Cindy thanked the chap and ended the call whereupon she began to cry.

"If Paul has his own mind in my body, then he's going to contact you, Cindy. I'm reasonably sure of it. That's what I'd do if I were in his strange situation. The only difference between his situation and mine is that I had you and Donnie to inform me of whose body I was occupying. All Paul has to go on is my wallet and sports bag."

My reassurance calmed Cindy down.

"While we wait for Paul to call, I need to learn about his job. Donnie, will you tell me all you can remember about what your Dad did at work when you were with him? Cindy, when Paul calls, I need to speak with him. Maybe we can solve this mystery together and get ourselves reunited with our own bodies."

CHAPTER 5 (Shocking Discovery)

Paul Skelding woke up and immediately sensed that something was wrong.

To begin with, he ached all over and his vision was blurry.

He eased himself off the bed and realized that he was in a strange room wearing pajamas that didn't belong to him.

Paul tried to recall his last memory.

He was home and Cindy was already in bed but not asleep. Paul changed into his pajama bottom and tee-shirt before joining Cindy.

They kissed goodnight and she asked if Paul could take Donnie somewhere the next day because their son was getting bored being stuck in the house so much. The pandemic had shut down most activities and Donnie's school chums were forbidden by their parents to mingle with anyone outside their home bubble.

Paul had quickly drifted off to sleep.

Someone must have kidnapped him in the night and brought him here, wherever "here" happened to me. Were Cindy and Donnie also taken?

His lips curled back in distaste as he noticed the deplorable state of this room. There was hideous wallpaper on each wall and the ratty old carpet was inundated with cigarette burns.

There wasn't even a phone in the room but Paul spotted a small sign on the inside of the door.

He limped over and read the sign.

This was a hotel and the sign contained the maximum daily room rate as well as a small chart showing this room's location in relation to the available exits.

How did Paul get from his own home to this dumpy hotel?

He wandered into the bathroom at which point the mystery deepened and took a definite detour into Weirdsville.

Paul's jaw gaped open as he looked in the mirror and saw an old man staring back at him.

The shock caused Paul to gasp and then to vomit into the toilet bowl.

Nothing made any sense and suddenly Paul realized that he had a massive headache. His mind must be playing tricks on him. Perhaps the kidnappers had injected him with some new form of hallucinogenic drug.

Unsure about absolutely everything, Paul ran a bath in order to get cleaned up and assess his situation. While the water was filling the tub, Paul went back into the room and looked around.

Some clothes were draped over a small chair in the corner of the room.

Paul rifled through the pockets but found nothing.

He had no clues about where he was or who he was.

Paul looked out the window and saw vague shapes of buildings but nothing was familiar to him. He could be almost anywhere.

It was so overwhelming.

Paul returned to the bathroom and climbed into the bathtub.

He closed his eyes and tried to get oriented.

This was too realistic to be a bad drug-induced trip. Something far more complex was going on.

Paul had seen the occasional movie about body-switching. He specifically recalled Family Man with Nicolas Cage.

That prompted Paul to wonder if this weak old carcass was actually him in the future but he discarded that notion. There was nothing even remotely similar in the facial structure or physical frame.

Paul was six feet three inches in height and weighed about 240 pounds. The body he was currently lugging around was at least three inches shorter and demonstrated no evidence whatsoever of ever having borne a muscular frame.

This was definitely somebody else's body.

That conclusion led to the issue of why Paul had been transported into this old man's body.

He finished his bath, dried himself off and then went back into the main room.

The clothes on the chair fit him so at least Paul was now dressed and could explore outside this room unless he was locked inside as a prisoner.

He began examining the contents of the dresser drawers, all of which were empty. The night-table was also empty except for a Gideon Bible.

Paul rifled through it but found no messages.

He got down on his hands and knees and looked under the bed. There was something there and he managed to grasp it and pull it out.

It was a sports bag.

Paul eagerly opened the bag and laid out the contents on the bed. There were more clothes, an electric razor and a small container which held a toothbrush, toothpaste, some small bandages, a bottle of Tylenol pain pills, a small knife, fork and spoon as well as a pair of nail scissors.

There was also a notebook and pen but nothing had been written inside.

Paul felt around in the sports bag and discovered another small leather bag. It contained a man's wallet and a passport.

Carefully Paul looked over each item.

The American passport had been issued in 2017 in the name of Peter Montrose who was born on July 26th, 1947. There were no customs stamps in the document which meant that Montrose hadn't travelled since obtaining the passport.

The address shown was an apartment in Ogdensburg, New York. That must be where Paul was now.

The wallet contained an American birth certificate showing the same birthdate as the passport and a bank card.

There was a fair amount of American cash and three business cards indicating that Peter Montrose was an attorney in Ogdensburg.

Another small slip of paper proclaimed that Montrose was a member of the Ogdensburg Duplicate Bridge Club but the small card was for 2018.

There was no driver's license or other piece of identification.

This old body was seventy-three. No wonder Paul felt so many aches and pains and had rotten eyesight.

The final bits and pieces of evidence were not helpful. There was a small photograph of an older lady and a business card from an optometrist in Ogdensburg.

Paul took the passport into the bathroom and confirmed that he was now the spitting image of the old guy pictured therein.

Despite a few misgivings, Paul cleaned the toothbrush and razor thoroughly before using the items on his face and mouth.

Apparently Peter Montrose didn't carry around a cell phone or even wear a watch. How did the old man figure out what time it was?

Paul packed up the sports bag and tried the door. It opened and Paul found himself in a grungy hallway.

The elevator bore a sign that it was out of order but Paul found the stairs and descended.

At the bottom he discovered that he was near the exit door but Paul went in the opposite direction and found a man working alone in a large men's beverage room.

He elicited as much information as he dared from the chap and learned that today was August 27th, 2020 and that Paul was now in Syracuse, New York, having checked in to this hotel yesterday afternoon.

That piece of information answered one pressing question.

Paul hadn't been kidnapped. The switch of bodies must have occurred sometime in the night.

Paul left the hotel in search of a pay phone.

On the way he spotted a drug store where Paul purchased a phone card which would make it so much easier to phone Cindy.

The clerk advised Paul of the location of a pay phone a block away.

Paul found it and used the phone card to call home, his own home.

CHAPTER 6 (The Phone Call)

Cindy's smart phone buzzed shortly before noon. She answered it immediately but put the call on speaker mode.

"Hello. This is Cindy Skelding."

"Cindy, please don't hang up on me. This is Paul but something absolutely bizarre has happened. Are you and Donnie okay?"

"Yes we are, Paul. Did you wake up to find yourself in an elderly man's body?"

"How could you possibly know that?"

"That man woke up this morning in our house but in your body. He's here with me now and needs to speak with you."

"What's going on?" Paul asked incredulously.

"As you've already figured out, I'm Peter Montrose and I've got absolutely no idea what happened to us. Cindy, Donnie and I have been discussing the matter. The only thing we could come up with is that whatever entity switched our bodies did so for a valid reason. Either I'm supposed to accomplish something in your life or vice versa. As much as I like feeling young again, I want to get back into my own body. We have to assume that we'll get reunited as soon as we've completed our assignment."

"At least that gives us something to base our actions on. Have you got any concrete ideas about what we need to do?"

"I do not. My own life is pretty mundane so I can't imagine why you are temporarily occupying my body other than the fact that your mind had to be stuck somewhere while I do whatever it is in your job that for some reason you are unable to do yourself."

"I can't imagine what that might be. I'm not a high level civil servant. At the moment I'm acting as an aide and bodyguard to a Congresswoman from Georgia but I'm only there temporarily. In fact

I've only been working for Carrie Brown for the past two months."

"Donnie has been filling me in a bit about your job from the two days that he tagged along with you last month. It must be that my legal training is needed in order to spot something terribly amiss that you wouldn't be able to notice yourself. Can you think of any area of your job that might fit the bill?"

"I can't."

"Perhaps it's something that I'm expected to notice while I'm working in your place. I'll just have to play it by ear."

"What am I supposed to do while you're being me?"

"You may as well travel here to Washington. Perhaps we need to put our heads together and analyze your job before we can figure out what we're supposed to do."

"I'll try to book a flight. If that's impossible then I'll take a bus to Washington."

Paul filled me in on his daily routine and provided me with his office computer passwords.

Then he chatted with Cindy and Donnie.

The boy thought this was the neatest thing he had ever seen.

Paul promised to keep in touch each day and he wished me luck in discerning whatever aspect of his work required this unique type of solution.

CHAPTER 7 (Imposter Bodyguard)

When the phone call ended, I went upstairs to shower and dress. Paul used a straight razor to shave but I'd always used an electric razor.

Cindy took Donnie and drove to a store to purchase an electric shaver for me as well as a toothbrush. I didn't want to use another man's toothbrush and I didn't want to show up for work with cuts all over my face and neck.

When they returned I got to work studying up on Paul Skelding. I needed to memorize his date of birth and learn as much as possible about his education and career. Paul at age thirty-three was forty years younger than me.

Cindy showed me photos of Carrie Brown and her principal aide and other staff.

It was a lot to take in but it was crucial that I learn as much as possible so as not to be outed as an imposter.

Cindy drove Donnie and me to Paul's place of work so at least I'd know a bit about the layout of the building. We couldn't go inside.

Tomorrow morning she would drive me to work.

Cindy and Paul's baby was due in November.

At suppertime the three of us talked about my life and theirs.

Paul called again at seven o'clock.

He had been unsuccessful in booking a flight from Syracuse to Washington because most of the flights weren't running. The few buses in operation were already fully booked.

His only option had been to purchase a bus ticket to New York City but his bus wouldn't depart until tomorrow evening at seven o'clock.

Paul was heading back to the Quinte Hotel to book a room for tonight.

Once he arrived in the Big Apple just before midnight tomorrow, he hoped to be able to find a bus or a train to Washington leaving the following morning.

I studied up some more on Paul Skelding later in the evening and crawled into bed in the spare bedroom at ten o'clock.

Despite being in a young man's body, my mind was exhausted from the sheer enormity of the situation.

On Friday morning the alarm clock woke me at six-thirty. Cindy made breakfast for the three of us and then Donnie accompanied us while Cindy drove me to work.

I was exceedingly nervous because I now had a firearm strapped to my waist.

It would be just my luck if today was set aside for a surprise marksmanship drill. I didn't even know which end the bullet fired out of.

Fortunately Congresswoman Carrie Brown was a total nobody in the huge American government.

Her office was in a converted building not particularly close to the bosom of government. Also, although she was a Democrat and her party controlled the House of Representatives, Carrie appeared to have little in the way of actual responsibilities. She was just an unimportant cog in a massive piece of machinery.

Paul had even less to do. In addition to accompanying Ms. Brown as a security measure, he did next to nothing else. Occasionally Paul was given a menial job such as addressing thank-you cards or requests for donations but for the most part he just sat around and waited for Carrie Brown to be on the move so that he could protect her.

Paul had mentioned wryly that Ms. Brown wasn't important enough to require security but that position was in the budget so had to be utilized or else the money for it would be sucked back into the government's coffers.

There was virtually no security at the main building entrance or beyond.

A lone guard smiled at me and said hello as I walked in. There was no metal detector or physical examination of any sort.

Cindy had provided me with a drawing of the building showing where Carrie Brown's office was located on the second floor.

I took the stairway there rather than the elevator and had no difficulty finding my own tiny office which I shared with a young intern named Astrid Brownell.

Carrie Brown's principal aide was a middle-aged Black woman named Blanche Carver who had her own private office adjoining the Congresswoman's office.

Astrid hadn't arrived yet but Blanche stuck her head out the door and bade me good morning.

"Carrie's flight is scheduled to arrive at Dulles at three o'clock this afternoon. The driver will pick you up at one o'clock sharp at the front door. Carrie doesn't have any appointments today which means she can proceed directly to her apartment. After Carrie is secured there, then the driver will take you home."

"I understand. What would you like me to do from now until the driver arrives?"

"I've got nothing for you. I guess you can assist Astrid with whatever she's doing."

Astrid strode in about two minutes before nine o'clock. As I had discerned from the photos Cindy had shown me, Astrid was also Black as was Carrie Brown herself.

Presumably Paul was only a temporary hire until such time as an African-American bodyguard and occasional assistant could be hired.

Astrid had no work for me which made the morning drag. I did log onto Paul's computer and examine the things he had been searching but nothing struck me as being tied to some nefarious plot to destroy America.

I concluded that the threat must lie elsewhere but it made no sense how my veteran legal mind could possibly be more attuned to anything related to security. That was Paul's specialty.

The driver, Elroy arrived precisely on time. I had been waiting outside for Elroy to show since twelve-thirty because I'd been so bored in the office twiddling my thumbs.

Paul had warned me that I wasn't allowed to sit up front with any driver unless Carrie was in the vehicle.

Elroy was a jovial middle-aged Black chap and we shot the breeze on the drive to Dulles International Airport.

He complained that it would have been a lot handier if Carrie had arrived at Ronald Reagan Airport rather than Dulles.

Elroy and I waited at the arrival area for Carrie Brown. She had brought no luggage so we didn't have to wait for any bags to be off-loaded from the aircraft.

I pretended to know what I was doing as bodyguard but in reality all I did was walk directly behind Ms. Brown who didn't speak with either of us.

She climbed in the back seat of the sedan and I sat up front with Elroy who raised the Plexiglas sound barrier so that our conversation wouldn't irritate the Congresswoman and also to prevent us from eavesdropping on her in case she used her smart phone during the journey.

When we arrived at Brown's residential building, I escorted her to the front entrance. I asked if she wanted me to check the interior of her apartment but she looked at me like I was insane while curtly declining my offer.

Elroy then drove me to Paul's house in a modest suburb of Washington. Again I sat in the back but we chatted about the ridiculous Covid-19 rules and restrictions.

Cindy and Donnie were waiting anxiously for me.

"Nothing struck me as remotely related to the destruction of America," I moaned. "It was a dreadfully boring day. Does Paul actually enjoy his job?"

"No he doesn't," Cindy responded. "Paul is hoping to get reassigned in the near future."

"Has Paul checked in yet?"

"No he hasn't. Donnie and I are starting to get worried."

"Maybe he'll call this evening. I'd like to talk to him again about his job. If today was any indication, then having an experienced set of legal eyes is a totally useless advantage relating to Paul's job. He doesn't do anything even remotely resembling classified work where I might spot some clue that he couldn't."

Donnie, Cindy and I sat down for supper.

Paul did phone shortly after supper. He had spent an uneventful day in Syracuse and was calling from the bus station where he expected to board his bus to New York City at seven o'clock.

I moaned that I had totally flamed out at Congresswoman Brown's office and didn't notice anything suspicious.

CHAPTER 8 (New York City)

After Paul called Cindy and Peter at seven o'clock on Thursday to apprise them of his lack of success in finding a bus leaving tonight or tomorrow morning, Paul purchased a submarine sandwich and a Pepsi and ate it back in his Room 404 at the Quinte Hotel.

He hoped that in the night he would be reunited with his own body in Washington and whisked away from this eerie nightmare.

His wishes didn't materialize and Paul found himself still in the old man's body on Friday morning.

It was a long day of waiting until his bus departed at seven o'clock on Friday evening.

Paul phoned Cindy from the bus depot and was discouraged to learn that Peter Montrose also had struck out today in spotting whatever catastrophe they were presumably supposed to prevent.

Paul found the bus ride to New York City tedious but at least it gave him a chance to ponder the strange events.

It seemed highly unlikely that anything having to do with his job working for Congresswoman Brown could require an experienced legal mind to spot some anomaly.

Paul was nothing more than a security guard with a rather mundane temporary assignment. His other duties at the government office were absolutely insignificant.

Perhaps the old lawyer was completely off with his analysis of why their bodies had been switched. In fact it was more accurate to say that their minds had been switched since their physical bodies had remained in their original place.

After a while he dozed off after saying a brief prayer requesting an immediate return of his mind back to his own body and his own life.

When Paul woke up, the bus was still travelling in the darkness. The nap had sharpened his mind which now allowed him to think more clearly. Earlier the strangeness of his predicament had overwhelmed him. By focusing on the mind switch as opposed to the body switch, the assignment, assuming there actually was one, could be looked at from a different angle.

Paul's job was so lacking in importance right now that the presence of an experienced legal mind in Paul's body didn't make much practical sense. No one was likely to harm Congresswoman Carrie Brown. She had no political power or enemies whatsoever.

What if it was Paul's mind that was required in Peter Montrose's tired old body in order to deal with some crucial situation?

Paul evaluated his past life for some possible clue.

The assignment couldn't be a physical one because Paul's mind

was stuck in a feeble and almost useless body.

Therefore Paul's proficiency in martial arts now seemed irrelevant.

His tours of duty in Afghanistan mostly involved stints with the bomb squad, studying explosive techniques and learning how to spot and dismantle assorted varieties of bombs.

That was something to ponder and Paul needed to be on the alert for suspicious activity.

Paul's security work after he returned from his second and final tour of duty didn't seem particularly promising as constituting the reason for the mind switch. So far his placements had been quite boring, culminating in his current uninspiring assignment.

Paul also needed to watch out for possible assassination attempts right now. His experience as a security officer and bodyguard could permit Paul to spot a dangerous situation in the

unlikely event that he happened to be in close proximity to a top-level politician on his journey from Syracuse to Washington.

Paul's attention drifted to other areas. The stench of body odor was rampant on this bus. The old man's sense of smell was certainly much more sensitive than Paul's was.

The obnoxious odors made for a very uncomfortable experience.

When the coach finally arrived in New York City shortly before midnight, Paul was disheartened to learn that there were no available buses heading to Washington until tomorrow afternoon.

Paul weighed his options.

He could take a cab to Penn Station and check out Amtrak trains to Washington or he could purchase a bus ticket and wait around for half a day.

Paul decided on the bus option. He bought his ticket and used the washroom facilities.

He had intended to wait in this station overnight but that plan was thwarted when an announcement on the loudspeaker informed the public that the Port Authority Terminal in Manhattan would be closing in five minutes.

That prompted Paul to think a bit more clearly.

If Paul had been placed in New York City in order to prevent some catastrophe, then he needed to be proactive. Sitting around this station for thirteen hours would have accomplished nothing.

Perhaps circumstances were being tweaked to lead Paul to where he was supposed to be.

Paul ventured out into the night to increase the odds of being in the right place at the right time.

He began walking north toward Central Park.

Being an old white-haired gentleman definitely made Paul vulnerable to trouble, especially so late on a Friday night.

He was unable to walk quickly and his rather pronounced limp illuminated him as weak and a promising robbery target. Carrying the sports bag branded Paul as a lost tourist in the eyes of any night predators.

Was this somehow an integral part of some grand plan? It didn't seem likely.

CHAPTER 9 (Lost Wallet)

After perhaps a dozen blocks, Paul arrived at the south entrance to Central Park.

There were very few pedestrians or vehicles in view and signs indicated that the park was closed to the public from one o'clock in the morning until six o'clock.

It was twenty minutes before one o'clock early on Saturday morning.

Paul entered the park, walked a short distance and then found a bench on which to sit and briefly contemplate his strategy.

Getting mugged couldn't possibly be part of the grand plan. Paul was clearly visible on the bench because an overhead lamp drenched the area in light.

He pulled out his bus ticket along with a pamphlet he had picked up at the bus station setting out the scheduled buses to Washington, D.C.

While Paul was examining the pamphlet, a gust of wind came out of nowhere and blew the pamphlet and bus ticket right out of his hands and into a cluster of nearby bushes.

Paul grabbed his sports bag to prevent its theft and stumbled into the bushes to find his ticket.

A tiny shaft of light illuminated a piece of paper under a bush. Paul reached in and almost grasped the paper but it was just out of his reach.

With great difficulty Paul got down on his hands and knees and poked his head, shoulders and arms further into the bushes.

The piece of paper he had spotted was in fact his bus ticket. Paul got hold of it and then peered around in the dimly lit underbrush looking for the bus schedule pamphlet.

His feeble eyes were relatively efficient to see nearby items. Although the pamphlet was nowhere to be found, Paul's eyes focused on another object.

He crawled a bit further into the bushes and discovered a man's wallet.

Retreating out of the undergrowth, Paul put his bus ticket into his own pocket and carried the sports bag back to the bench.

The wallet was full of cash, credit cards and a tiny thumb-drive.

There was no telephone number listed in the wallet but there was a New York State driver's license showing an address on 721 Fifth Avenue here in the city.

Paul pondered this development.

It might be sheer coincidence but it was just as likely to be a crucial step in the grand plan.

Paul left the park and realized that Fifth Avenue was right around the corner.

He walked across the street and quickly found the building at 721 Fifth Avenue. It was the famous Trump Tower building.

Paul located the main entrance. There was no exterior doorman at this time of night but a security guard was stationed just inside the door.

Paul gestured for him to come outside.

The guard was a bit hesitant but did poke his head out the door.

"What can I do for you, sir?"

"I was sitting in Central Park a few minutes ago and happened to find a man's wallet belonging to someone who resides in this building. I wanted to return it to the owner or at least at this late hour have you inform the owner that I'm in possession of his wallet and can bring it around tomorrow morning."

"Whose wallet is it?"

"The name on the identification is Gerhard Bruhnsmon in Suite 4703."

"Are you a vagrant?"

"Actually I'm a retired attorney but I've been stuck on a smelly bus for many hours."

The security guard smiled.

"In that case come on in and I'll contact the owner for you."

The guard phoned up to the suite. After a very short pause, he began talking into the phone.

"I'm so sorry to disturb you at this very late hour, sir. There's a gentleman in the lobby who claims to have found your wallet in Central Park."

Paul couldn't hear the response but it appeared that the guard was on hold.

After a delay of two or three minutes, the guard said, "I'll bring him up to your suite, sir."

The guard addressed Paul.

"You'll have to sign in first but then I'll escort you up to the suite."

While Paul was signing in, the guard rapped on a door behind the concierge counter and another guard emerged.

"Look after the entrance while I take this chap upstairs, Byron."

Paul followed the guard to the elevators and they rode up to the 47th floor. The escort rapped lightly on the door to Suite 4703 and a middle-aged man in a suit opened the door.

"Good evening, Mr. Bruhnsmon. This is the gentleman who found your wallet. I've checked his own ID and confirmed that he is legitimate. His name is Peter Montrose and he is a retired attorney from Upstate New York."

"Thank you, Blake. I'll escort Mr. Montrose out of the complex once our business is completed. Please come in, Mr. Montrose."

The security guard replied, "Very good, sir. Goodnight."

Bruhnsmon ushered Paul inside and closed the door on Blake.

Paul extracted the lost wallet from his pocket and handed it to the gentleman without commenting.

"I didn't even realize that I had lost my wallet. It must have happened while I was walking my dog in the park a couple of hours ago. Where did you find it?"

"My bus ticket blew out of my hand in a gust of wind and I had to crawl under some bushes to retrieve it."

"That's interesting. Patches was a naughty boy tonight and briefly escaped my control. I also had to crawl under some bushes to grab his leash which had gotten tangled in some underbrush."

"I'm just glad that I found it for you, sir. Please verify that all the contents are accounted for at which point I'll say goodnight and be on my way."

CHAPTER 10 (Imposter Attorney)

Bruhnsmon rifled through his wallet and seemed thrilled when he came across the thumb-drive.

"I'm so pleased that this didn't get lost in the shuffle. It contains a ton of very confidential information. Please let me reward you for your honesty."

"That isn't necessary, sir. I couldn't accept a reward for doing the right thing."

"Didn't Blake tell me that you were a lawyer?"

"That's correct."

"I don't believe you."

Paul's jaw gaped open. What could he have possibly said that gave away the fact that he was an imposter attorney?

Then it dawned on Paul.

Mr. Bruhnsmon might somehow be part of the grand plan.

Suddenly Bruhnsmon burst out laughing.

"I was attempting to crack a joke, Peter. Every attorney I've ever met wouldn't turn down money for any reason. I'm a lawyer myself as well as a forensic analyst. What type of law did you practice?"

Paul had no idea how to answer. Peter Montrose hadn't told him anything about his life as an attorney. He'd only been interested in learning about Paul's life.

"It wasn't a tough question, Peter. Is there more to you than meets the eye?"

"That's the understatement of the year," Paul blurted out.

"Do you want to tell me about it? I've got an extremely logical and open mind. Sorting out your problem might be a satisfactory way for me to repay you for returning my wallet."

"I don't know whether I'm even allowed to tell you."

"I'm not following you. Can you be more specific?"

"I'm so far out of my comfort zone right now. I think it would be safer if you just escorted me back outside. My role in the grand plan seems to be extremely minor. All I'm expected to do is travel to Washington. Mr. Montrose is the one tasked with spotting the anomaly."

"Aren't you Peter Montrose?"

"This is his body but his mind is occupying my body back in Washington. I'm Paul Skelding."

Mr. Bruhnsmon looked at Paul like he was a nut-job. Paul realized that it had been a mistake blurting out as much as he just did.

"I've said more than enough, Mr. Bruhnsmon. Please call Blake to retrieve me or escort me down to the lobby yourself."

"I think you need psychiatric help, Peter or Paul, whoever you believe you are."

"I need something, that's for sure."

The two men were silent for a moment. During the lull Paul

became rather miffed with this arrogant rich guy who had just insulted him.

"At least you've discovered something new about yourself, Mr. Bruhnsmon."

"And what might that be?"

"You might be logical but you certainly don't have an open mind. It's obvious that my situation is way beyond your pay grade. Take me down to the lobby right now."

"That's an interesting comment. Before we leave, provide me with a bit of tangible proof. Perhaps you can convince me to expand my perspective."

Paul thought about Bruhnsmon's request.

"The only possible verification I can think of would be for us to call my wife in Washington and have her wake Peter Montrose up so that he can speak with us."

"It's the middle of the night."

"I'm not crazy about the idea either but it's the only area of corroboration possible. I wouldn't even suggest it except that finding your wallet appeared perhaps to have been orchestrated rather than mere coincidence."

"What difference would that make?"

"It could mean that you've become a pawn in the grand plan."

"What grand plan?"

"Peter Montrose believes that our bodies were switched by some unknown entity for a critical reason. Our role in the grand plan is determining what it is that Peter and I are supposed to do. In actual fact, although Peter terms it a body switch, really it was our minds that were exchanged. His body remained in Syracuse and mine is still at my home in Washington."

"If I understand you correctly, Peter is the attorney but you're now stuck in his body. Who is Paul Skelding?"

"I'm a security guard and assistant aide to Congresswoman Carrie Brown from Georgia. I reside in a suburb of Washington with my pregnant wife Cindy and our eleven year old son, Donnie. Peter intended to work my shift yesterday. He is convinced that he has been put into my body to work my job in Washington in order to uncover some horrible plot to do something critically harmful. Peter believes that it must be his legal experience which is necessary to spot the plot and stop it. He believes that my role in his body is simply as a temporary vessel for his old body."

"Let's make the call."

Paul punched in his home phone number. It rang four times before a groggy Cindy picked up.

"Cindy, it's me. I'm fine but it's important that I speak with Peter. Will you please wake him up? Then you can put the phone on speaker mode and I'll do the same here."

Paul handed the fancy phone to Bruhnsmon who pressed the correct button to enable both of them to hear the conversation.

While Cindy went down the hallway to Peter's room, she asked Paul where he was.

"I'm in New York City at the apartment of a gentleman I just met. I've purchased a bus ticket to Washington but it doesn't depart until early Saturday afternoon. That was the only available transportation."

They heard Cindy waking up Peter Montrose. A moment later they were all on a mini-conference call.

CHAPTER 11 (Recruiting an Ally)

I was shaken awake by Cindy Skelding.

In my confusion I had no idea what time it was.

"What's wrong, Cindy?" I mumbled.

"Paul is calling from New York City and needs to speak with you right away. I'll put the phone on speaker so we can both listen."

"Hello Paul. I'm awake now. What's happening?"

"I'm in a New York City apartment with a gentleman named Gerhard Bruhnsmon. I've explained our strange situation to him and he insisted that he needed to talk to you before deciding whether to help us decipher what it is that we're supposed to do."

Paul explained to me the circumstances leading to his meeting Bruhnsmon along with Paul's belief that perhaps the gentleman might be some part of the grand plan.

"It can't hurt," I responded. "What do you want to know, Mr. Bruhnsmon? As Paul already informed you, he and I have had our bodies switched but we're floundering around trying to make sense of the situation."

"Are you really an attorney?"

"I am but I retired in April after forty-seven years running my own legal office."

"The old chap here in my apartment showed me the business cards and birth certificate in his wallet a few moments ago and he also let me look at his passport. The old fellow here is Peter Montrose."

"He's Peter Montrose in body only. We can't fathom why our bodies were switched on the night of August 26th while we slept in completely different cities. Our assumption is that it's happened for a reason. Paul seems to believe that you might be able to assist us in finding the answer."

"What do you think?"

"I'm willing to include you in our quest. It can't hurt. My initial reasoning was that my legal experience inserted into Paul's body was the likely reason for the switch. I felt that perhaps I would recognize some huge threat related to his job in Washington that Paul would be unable to discern. Yesterday I assumed Paul's identity and worked his shift but discovered that Paul's job is very mundane. Absolutely nothing popped up in which my legal knowledge would even be relevant. I'm hoping that today might be different but I'm not optimistic."

"Were you in Ogdensburg when your bodies were switched?"

"No, I was in Syracuse on the first day of an extended bus journey. I vacated my apartment in Ogdensburg, gave away my furniture and left my home town for parts unknown. I had a bit of a premonition that my days were numbered and my trip was to be my farewell performance until my ill health ended my time on Earth."

"Have your physical ailments followed you into Paul's body?"

"No they haven't. It's pleasant being young and healthy again but I want my old body back so that I can get on with my own life. Cindy is beside herself with worry although their son Donnie believes that it's a great adventure."

"Did you not own a vehicle?"

"My old car died on me a year ago and a week later my optometrist yanked my driver's license because of my rapidly deteriorating eyesight."

"Despite having been an attorney for so many decades, are you now short of money?"

"No, I'm quite well off. My wife died in 1999 and we had no children. I haven't even dated since Deidre passed away. I am however rather frugal and never wasted money on fancy cars."

"What sort of assistance do you hope to receive from me?"

"I expect nothing unless a fresh set of eyes can discover something that Paul and I have missed."

"At the moment my logical mind is unable to overcome its disbelief concerning your alleged situation. I'm so sorry. If some epiphany strikes me, then I'll contact you. It's very late and I'm going to escort the old gentleman here with me out of the building. Do you have any questions for him before we end this call?"

I asked Paul if he had come across any potential basis for the grand plan but he responded that the only unusual event had been his discovery of the lost wallet.

We discussed that issue for a few minutes but concluded that it was likely a red herring and totally unrelated to our mission.

Cindy spoke with Paul for a moment and she promised to maintain a positive attitude for Donnie's sake. Paul said that he'd probably be back in Washington by late Saturday evening assuming that the bus was on time and that he'd grab a taxi home as soon as he arrived.

We ended the call and I went back to sleep.

CHAPTER 12 (Acrid Smell)

Mr. Bruhnsmon put his smart phone back in his pocket.

"I'll admit that it was a fascinating conversation but I'm totally perplexed about the entire matter. You were correct when you commented that it would be above my pay grade. All I can suggest is that you keep your eyes and ears open for any clues and hope that the man we just spoke with can solve your dilemma for you."

"At least you listened to Peter Montrose and now we've had another set of eyes evaluate our situation. You may as well escort me down to the lobby and I'll be on my way."

"Where will you go?"

"I'll walk back to the Port Authority Bus Terminal and wait for my bus to Washington."

"It's too dangerous to walk at night in New York. The defunding of the police departments has drastically increased the crime rate. I've got one of the few parking spots available in the underground garage here. Since you found my wallet, it's the least I can do to drive you to the bus terminal."

"I'm happy to accept the ride, Mr. Bruhnsmon. Although I'm a martial arts expert and an Afghanistan war veteran, I doubt that my skills would be particularly effective housed in Peter's old body."

Bruhnsmon locked up his apartment and they took the elevator down to the parking level.

"I'm fortunate to have a parking spot for my Mercedes. Spaces are severely limited in Manhattan in general and at Trump Tower in particular."

Paul had never seen such expensive automobiles in one place.

"This parking garage is amazing. Look at all the Rolls-Royces and Bentleys."

"The residents are extremely wealthy."

Paul saw an electrician's van parked in a space just up ahead and couldn't refrain from making a joke.

"I've heard that electricians in New York City earn big bucks but I wouldn't have expected any of them to rip folks off to the extent that they could afford to live here."

"They can't. One of the residents must be having renovations done. I'm surprised that the condo management has authorized overnight work to be carried out. We have very strict noise rules in this building."

As they passed the van, Paul got a whiff of an acrid but familiar odor.

"Do you smell that?" Paul asked Bruhnsmon.

"I don't smell anything."

"That's the stench that the explosive C-4 gives off. It must be coming from the electrician's van."

"How would you know that?"

"I worked bomb details during my tours in Afghanistan. We've got to get into that van right now."

Paul ran to the van but the doors were all locked. The van was windowless except at the front. Paul peered inside but there was a drop cloth hanging just behind the front seats which prevented him from seeing what was in the storage area of the vehicle.

"Do you have a tire iron and a flashlight in your car?" he barked at Bruhnsmon.

"Yes."

"Bring them to me right away and call 911."

Bruhnsmon ran ahead to his Mercedes, retrieved the requested items and quickly returned them to the old man.

As Bruhnsmon called 911, the old fellow with the Peter Montrose identification pried open the rear door of the van.

"Holy shit! This is the biggest bomb I've ever seen," Paul shouted as he climbed up into the van and shone the flashlight around.

He located the timer and was crushed when he saw that the massive device was timed to explode in seven minutes.

"Mr. Bruhnsmon, this thing is going to blow in a few minutes. Get in here and bring me my sports bag."

Bruhnsmon did as he was instructed despite a strong urge to run like Hell.

Paul ripped open the sports bag and found the small shaving kit containing the nail scissors.

"Try to keep the flashlight steady," he snapped at Bruhnsmon whose hand was shaking wildly while he shone the light on the timing device.

All of Paul's training and experience came out to play as he calmly assessed the design of the timer and began to snip the key wires in the proper progression.

The only impediment was that these old man's hands weren't as strong as Paul's which made it a bit more difficult to cut the wires using such a flimsy tool.

As the timer dropped to two minutes, Paul had the sudden worry that he wasn't going to be able to defuse the bomb in time.

A strange thought popped into his mind. Would Peter Montrose be blown to smithereens in this opulent parking garage? If that happened, would Paul wake up in his own bed in the morning and learn about this terrorist act on the news?

Despite the dread that filled his very soul, Paul continued to methodically cut the wires.

Finally with just forty-seven seconds remaining on the timer, the final wire was snipped and the timer went dark.

"Were you successful?" Bruhnsmon barked nervously.

"We'll find out in less than a minute. I've decommissioned the timer but it's still possible that the trigger has been activated."

The two men were deathly silent and perfectly still for at least three minutes.

Nothing happened.

Paul had successfully defused the huge bomb.

CHAPTER 13 (Aftermath)

"We did it," Paul finally whispered breathlessly.

They climbed out of the van.

"How can we explain anything to the police?" Paul asked his new friend. "Peter Montrose is a retired attorney and wouldn't have a clue how to defuse a bomb. Nobody will believe the real story about the body switch."

They heard rapidly approaching sirens.

Bruhnsmon pondered the dilemma for a moment before responding.

"You'll need to marry up Peter Montrose and Paul Skelding in another way but I'm too shaky at this precise moment to think straight."

"The only thing I can think of is that the two of us are friends and that Paul taught Peter about bomb defusing techniques over the telephone. Can you live with that story?"

"It's not foolproof but it sure beats the truth. Take this bit of basic legal advice from me. Don't provide any more details than absolutely necessary."

The police poured into the parking garage. Paul thought that was rather incompetent given the fact that he had heard Mr. Bruhnsmon inform the 911 operator that a suspected bomb had been found in an electrician's van in the parking garage of Trump Tower.

Paul waved at the police to approach the van.

A well-dressed man introduced himself as Detective Moe Enright and almost fainted when he glanced inside the van.

Paul explained quickly.

"I'm pretty sure we successfully defused this device but there's a ton of powerful explosives inside the vehicle. The van should be removed from this parking garage as quickly and safely as possible."

"What were you fellows doing in the parking garage at this hour of the night and how did you discover what was inside this vehicle?"

Bruhnsmon replied.

"I'm Gerhard Bruhnsmon and this is Peter Montrose. I was about to give Mr. Montrose a ride to the bus station. That deep burgundy Mercedes right over there is my car. I reside in this building. Mr. Montrose smelled what he thought was something he called C-4 explosive as we walked near this van. He pried the doors open with the tire iron from my automobile and discovered that his nose was right. He defused the device while I shone my flashlight on the timing mechanism."

"Well done, Mr. Montrose. Look, we'd better get you chaps out of here while we decide what to do about the explosives."

Paul realized that the lie had now been set. No doubt the investigators would have a million questions. Paul needed to keep his story simple and not deviate from the basic facts he and Bruhnsmon had already admitted.

Bruhnsmon and Paul were whisked away in separate police vehicles to the Manhattan precinct.

CHAPTER 14 (Interrogation)

Paul was escorted into a relatively large conference room where video equipment was set up.

Some very high profile law enforcement types assembled in the room within ten minutes of Paul's arrival.

Absolutely no one was wearing a face mask.

The attendees introduced themselves. Some were from the FBI, some from NYPD and one chap named Colonel Ronald McDonald was an explosives expert now working for Homeland Security but formerly with the US Army.

The initial questions were friendly and routine, requesting very basic information about Peter Montrose's identity and background.

Paul's responses must have triggered some suspicion because the tone shifted from pleasant to accusatory.

Fortunately Paul had suffered through numerous de-briefings in Afghanistan after various assignments and didn't allow himself to be intimidated.

"What were you doing in Trump Tower at two o'clock in the morning of Saturday, the 29th of August, 2020?"

"My bus arrived from Syracuse shortly before midnight on Friday night. I purchased a ticket to Washington just before the Port Authority Terminal closed for the night. I walked to Central Park and sat on a bench in order to wait until one o'clock when the park closed up. My bus ticket was blown out of my hand and flew under a nearby bush. When I ducked into the bushes to pick it up, I found a man's wallet."

The interrogator interrupted Paul to have him pinpoint which bench he had sat on. Then he asked Paul to continue.

"The wallet was owned by Gerhard Bruhnsmon and his address was on his driver's license. I left the park and found the address which turned out to be Trump Tower. The security guard named Blake let me in and phoned Mr. Bruhnsmon who instructed Blake to escort me up to his Apartment 4703."

"Had you ever met Gerhard Bruhnsmon before?"

"No. The gentleman thanked me profusely for returning his wallet. He offered me a reward but I declined. We chatted for a while and I told Mr. Bruhnsmon that I was going to walk back to the bus terminal and wait for it to open. He said that it was too dangerous for an old man to walk in New York City alone at night and he insisted on driving me there."

"Had Blake woken up Mr. Bruhnsmon when he called his suite?"

"I don't believe so. Mr. Bruhnsmon was dressed in a suit when we got up to his apartment. When we reached the parking garage I was amazed at all the luxury automobiles. I saw the electrician's van up ahead and made a joke that I was surprised that an electrician could afford to live at Trump Tower."

"What was Mr. Bruhnsmon's response?"

"He said that one of the residents must be having renovations done which surprised him because the management was very strict about noise especially during the night. When we walked past the van I smelled C-4, informed Mr. Bruhnsmon and he retrieved the tire iron and a flashlight from his Mercedes. I pried open the rear doors of the van and discovered the bomb. The timer indicated that the device would explode in seven minutes. Together we defused it with only forty-seven seconds to spare."

The man from the army snapped at Paul.

"You're lying. C-4 can't be detected through a vehicle by a human nose. Even sniffer dogs have difficulty locating explosives in a closed-up vehicle."

"I've been cursed with an incredibly sensitive sense of smell. Mr. Bruhnsmon admitted that he couldn't smell anything but I sure could. I don't mean to insult anyone present in this room, but six of you reek of body odor including you Colonel McDonald. It's obvious that you had to rush to get here and had no time to shower before getting dressed."

Colonel McDonald blushed in embarrassment but Paul's comment didn't shut him up. He demanded to know where Paul had learned how to defuse a bomb.

"I'm a lawyer. It's my job to learn skills."

"We've checked your service records. You never even served in the military."

Paul recalled what Peter Montrose had admitted during one of the phone calls about his lack of experience with guns.

"Actually I've never operated nor even handled a firearm of any sort. I'm just a newly retired small town attorney who happened to remember how bombs work."

The rest of the interview involved complex questions from Colonel McDonald about bomb-making and the defusing of bombs. He knew much more about the craft than Paul did but at least Paul was able to persuade him that Peter Montrose was highly knowledgeable about the subject.

A clock on the wall revealed that it was now five-thirty in the morning. Thankfully the interview ended but an argument ensued.

The authorities tried to persuade Paul to remain as the city's guest in New York City for a day or two while they continued with their investigation.

Paul insisted that he had to get to Washington today and refused their offer.

For a few minutes Paul thought they were going to detain him as a material witness but presumably they realized that mistreating a hero would make for terrible media coverage.

As a concession, Paul had agreed to remain in the precinct for a few hours while the investigation continued.

He was taken to a much smaller room where Paul was provided with breakfast and the use of a washroom.

He was unable to shave because the police insisted on retaining his sports bag as evidence for the time being.

Detective Enright entered the room and sat with Paul after he had cleaned up a bit.

"You saved the city a truckload of chaos, Mr. Montrose. We just got word back that the van contained enough explosives to potentially cause the entire building to collapse."

"Hopefully you can also nail the perpetrator. With the van and bomb intact, there should be enough clues to quickly find out who was responsible."

"No information is being released to the media at this time. You'll be an overnight sensation once the details get leaked."

"That gives me all the more reason to leave New York City. I don't want to attract any attention to myself. I'm glad I was in the right place at the right time but I really want my identity to remain anonymous."

Enright attempted to make friendly conversation but Paul realized that the Detective was merely playing good cop in order to elicit information. Paul refused to play along.

CHAPTER 15 (Solving the Case)

With the combined resources of the FBI, NYPD and a myriad of other agencies, an army of assorted cops tackled this case of domestic terrorism.

Video surveillance tapes were gathered from the Port Authority Terminal, Central Park and Trump Tower itself.

Peter Montrose's arrival at the bus depot was quickly spotted and confirmed the information he had provided.

Similarly the cameras at Central Park had recorded Montrose's arrival in the park, his brief time on the park bench and even recorded that the bus ticket had been blown out of his hand and into some nearby bushes just as he had claimed.

Montrose was off camera while he crawled under the bushes but he emerged again on the film returning to the bench with a man's wallet in his grasp.

The investigators watched Montrose examine the contents of the wallet and then exit Central Park.

His route to 721 Fifth Avenue was fully caught at which point the Trump Tower surveillance confirmed that a security guard named Blake Conrad approached Montrose, let him enter the building's foyer and then after a phone call was made, the guard escorted Montrose into the elevator and up to Suite 4703.

At that point Gerhard Bruhnsmon was seen speaking with Conrad and Montrose. Conrad returned to the main foyer and Montrose entered Suite 4703.

About an hour later Bruhnsmon and Montrose left the suite and took the elevator to the underground parking level.

The cameras in the garage thereafter confirmed events precisely as both Montrose and Bruhnsmon had stated.

Blake Conrad had also been questioned and had verified his brief involvement with Montrose and then Bruhnsmon.

That aspect of the case was clear cut.

None of those three gentlemen were suspects and nothing more complex than immaculate timing had thwarted a diabolical terrorism attempt by the slimmest of margins.

Occasionally the forces of good got lucky.

The other avenues of exploration involved the electrical van and the occupants of the apartment in whose parking spot the van was parked.

Trump Tower's management were fastidious about security and it only took a couple of very early morning phone calls to confirm that Suite 3919 was rented with one interior underground parking space to a numbered company. The rent was $6,400 per month and the current tenant had only moved in at the beginning of July.

Suite 3919 had obtained permission from management for the completion of non-disturbing electrical renovations during the hours of eleven PM on Friday until six o'clock the following morning.

The name on the electrician's van turned out to be phony. There was no such business.

However the driver of the van was caught on the security camera entering the parking garage at twenty minutes before midnight on Friday evening.

The driver was alone and he simply exited the vehicle, locked it up and then proceeded to the elevators. Instead of riding up to the 39th floor, the man got off at the main level and left the building.

Fingerprints from the van led to the identification of Grant Justin who had been a security guard at a department store in Queen's for the past two years.

When police arrived at Justin's dumpy apartment in Queen's and announced their presence, a single gunshot rang out and then total silence.

Officers used a battering ram to enter the unit and found Mr. Justin freshly deceased. The man had taken his own life.

Investigators swarmed the apartment and quickly discovered handwritten diaries which recorded the ravings of a lunatic.

Apparently Mr. Justin had targeted Trump Tower because one of the doormen there had beaten out Justin for a promotion at the department store.

Justin had used most of his savings to form a numbered company and rent the suite in Trump Tower in order to carry out his act of revenge against a co-worker.

His motive made no sense to sane folks especially since that doorman wasn't even on duty at the time the explosion was set to detonate.

The FBI with the concurrence of the NYPD concluded that the explosive-filled van was the act of a deranged lone-wolf and quickly closed their investigation.

The entire time frame from the 911 call to the analysis of the diaries and the investigative conclusion took only ten and a half hours.

Word came down from the top not to release many of the details.

The media would not be informed of the close encounter with an unfathomable tragedy. They would simply be told that the NYPD had detected and defused a bomb in an underground parking garage and had quickly solved the crime. The name of the perpetrator would be released but few other details.

The last thing New York City needed in this time of coronavirus and economic devastation was to be frightened beyond belief by stories of domestic terrorism.

CHAPTER 16 (Free at Last)

At eleven o'clock on Saturday morning Detective Enright received a call on his smart phone.

He turned to Paul.

"You're free to go, Mr. Montrose. We've already found the perpetrator. He was a nut case out for revenge and committed suicide when the NYPD announced their presence at his apartment door."

"That's wonderful news, Detective Enright. Will someone drive me to the bus station?"

"I'll take you myself. It's the least I can do. Your sense of smell saved New York City from what would surely have been one of the worst cases on record of domestic terrorism. Your sports bag and contents have also been released as evidence and we can pick your stuff up at the front desk on our way out."

Once Enright dropped Paul off at the terminal entrance, Paul used his phone card to call Cindy.

"I'll be boarding the bus in about an hour, honey. It should arrive in Washington around seven o'clock and I'll grab a cab home. Is you-know-who working again today?"

"Yes he is but he should be home before you arrive."

"Tell him the grand plan has been accomplished. With any luck we'll switch back to normal while we sleep tonight."

"That would be so wonderful. I've been worried sick about both of you."

"I'll reveal all the gory details tonight. You'll be quite astounded. I was a busy old boy last night."

The bus departed on time and at quarter to seven on Saturday evening Paul arrived in Washington and caught a taxi home.

...

I began Paul's Saturday shift at nine o'clock in the morning. Just like yesterday, there was virtually nothing to occupy my time.

Congresswoman Brown arrived shortly after me and all I did for the entire day was wait around in case she needed me to accompany her anywhere.

She didn't require my services and spent the entire day holed up in her office.

Astrid mentioned that our boss was making phone calls all day for campaign donations since her seat was one of the ones up for election on November 3rd.

At four-thirty Elroy drove Carrie Brown home while I "protected" her from my spot on the front passenger seat.

Thereafter Elroy drove me to Paul's house.

I had been exceedingly bored all day because absolutely nothing occurred which could possibly have involved my legal expertise.

In fact I began to have doubts about the existence of some grand plan which had required the body switch in the first place.

It simply wasn't conceivable that I had missed some salient clue in the two boring days I had worked in Paul's job.

Cindy and Donnie were excited when I walked in their door.

"Dad's on his way home, Mr. Montrose and he told Mom that he's accomplished the mission. He thinks you'll be switched back to normal tonight."

"That's fantastic news, Donnie. I can't wait to hear about why it was necessary to switch our bodies. It certainly wasn't anything having to do with Paul's job working for the Congresswoman. I'm surprised that your Dad isn't brain-dead already. I feel like a zombie and I've only worked there for two insanely boring days."

Cindy made supper for the three of us because Donnie was hungry. She set aside a plate for Paul in case he hadn't eaten supper before he arrived home.

I was praying that Paul was correct in his assumption and that he and I would be reunited with our own bodies overnight as we slept.

Living in another man's skin had been most disconcerting.

CHAPTER 17 (Switch-Back)

Cindy, Donnie and I were glued to the front window after supper.

At twenty minutes past seven on Saturday evening, a taxi pulled up and Paul Skelding in my body climbed out and walked up the sidewalk to the front door.

It was the strangest sensation watching myself.

Paul and I shook hands when he walked in.

Donnie couldn't overcome the confusion. His young mind couldn't fathom that the white-haired old man who entered the home and spoke in a strange voice was actually his own father.

Paul decided that Donnie was old enough to be told the truth about what had occurred.

We sat in the living-room and Paul took us through the chronology since we had ended our last call in the wee hours of this strange Saturday morning.

Cindy burst into tears when Paul admitted how close he and Mr. Bruhnsmon had come to dying in the electrician's van.

Paul described in detail his interrogation at the police precinct. I needed to know as much as possible about that period because our fervent hope was that when I woke up tomorrow morning, I'd be back in my own body.

It was very possible that the police would want to question me further at some point before they closed their investigation.

Cindy and Donnie decided to go to bed at ten o'clock.

Paul and I sat up and discussed how we would handle future interrogations. Our feeling was that Paul and his family were well protected because the authorities had no idea that he was in any way involved.

As for me, I would have to refuse to answer any future questions on the matter. Paul tried to explain the rudiments of bomb defusing techniques but my legal mind was only comfortable with abstract concepts. Understanding how machines or bombs actually worked was far beyond my capabilities.

The fact that I was a nomad would go a long way to allowing me to avoid interrogation.

We briefly touched on the scenario wherein we didn't switch back to our own bodies but that door was too frightening to open.

At midnight we each went to a separate bedroom for the night. Paul understandably didn't want me either sleeping in or waking up in the same bed as his wife.

I really wasn't all that tired when I crawled into bed in the spare bedroom I'd been using. Until this evening's startling revelations, my entire day had been insufferably boring.

I put a small mirror on the bedside table so that tomorrow morning when I woke up, I wouldn't have to exit the bedroom and run to the bathroom to discover who I was.

For a while I relived the entire adventure in my mind and tried to sort out the ethical and spiritual ramifications of the freakish turn of events.

They were too complex to comprehend.

Eventually I did drift off to sleep.

On Sunday morning I woke up and with immense relief stared into the small mirror at a white-haired old fogey.

I leapt out of the bed, threw on Paul's dressing-gown and went to wake up the rest of the household.

Cindy and Donnie had slept in the same room. The weirdness of the situation last evening had made the young boy too afraid to sleep in his own room.

"Wake up, Cindy. Time to get up, Donnie. Peter Montrose is back in his own body. Let's go wake Paul up."

They scrambled out of bed and we literally ran to the basement level where Paul had slept in the pull-out sofa in the den.

Donnie jumped onto the mattress.

"Wake up, Dad. Wake up."

Paul's eyes opened and he smiled when he saw my old body standing at the foot of his bed.

He stood up and towered over me. Paul examined his arms and felt his face.

"Thank God we're back in our own bodies," he exclaimed.

Paul hugged his wife and daughter.

We adjourned to the kitchen where we shared a celebratory breakfast.

The sheer joy of this successful body switch-back permeated the household.

CHAPTER 18 (Contradictory Evidence)

For the first few hours immediately following the 911 call, the NSA and Homeland Security had been contacted to assist in the investigation.

When the FBI and the NYPD located the perpetrator and solved the case so quickly, those other agencies were duly informed and asked to stand down.

Since Gerhard Bruhnsmon was never a suspect, neither the FBI nor the NYPD even thought to check his phone records.

Neither did Homeland Security but the NSA did call up the details.

Stanley Walton, one of the weekend shift technicians, downloaded the phone records on Saturday afternoon and glanced over the results while reading the NSA's copy of the NYPD official report.

Two calls relevant to the incident time frame caught the technician's attention. One was actually mentioned in the police report and apparently occurred when the security guard in the main foyer of Trump Tower called up to the suite of Gerhard Bruhnsmon. That call commenced at fifteen minutes after one o'clock and lasted for three and a half minutes.

Not present in the police report was any mention of a second call from the suite to a Washington residence owned by Paul and Cynthia Skelding. That call began at thirty-two minutes past one o'clock and lasted for nine minutes.

That was highly suspicious because the bomb was discovered and the 911 call made a scant eight minutes later.

Walton called the NYPD lead detective, Moe Enright and reached the chap directly.

After introducing himself, Walton explained what he had just discerned from the phone records of Gerhard Bruhnsmon.

"We weren't aware of that call. Peter Montrose is on a bus heading to Washington right now. I know because I dropped him off at the bus station three hours ago. By any chance does a recording of that phone call exist?"

"If it does, it could only be accessed through Homeland Security or the FBI. The NYPD doesn't have access authority to any NSA recorded phone calls without a proper warrant having been issued."

"Colonel Ronald McDonald with Homeland Security sat in on the interrogation of Montrose. Would you contact him about your discovery? I'll leave it up to his discretion whether to obtain a copy of the actual call. As far as I'm concerned, the case has been solved."

Walton obtained McDonald's direct contact number from Detective Enright and called the Colonel immediately.

McDonald requested that an encrypted recording of the call be forwarded to his computer forthwith. Normally he wouldn't have bothered but it had irked him to be publicly embarrassed regarding his personal hygiene by the smart-ass attorney.

When he received the recording, Colonel McDonald was completely perplexed. The phone call appeared to be the ramblings of two lunatics trying to explain insanity to a third party, in this instance Gerhard Bruhnsmon.

Since the phone call had made no mention of the bomb, then it had no direct bearing on the case especially since the bomb maker had been caught and the case solved.

On further reflection, McDonald decided that in fact the phone call could be crucial to a proper understanding of the situation.

McDonald began searching Homeland's extensive records for Paul Skelding and discovered some intriguing information.

Skelding had served two tours in Afghanistan and was a qualified member of the bomb disposal unit in both tours of duty.

The Colonel replayed his copy of the interrogation of Peter Montrose with particular emphasis on the elderly lawyer's knowledge of bombs.

It defied belief that a small town lawyer with no military training could acquire such extensive knowledge of bomb making and the defusing of assorted varieties of bombs without practical training.

And yet the old fellow McDonald grilled in the NYPD precinct was highly knowledgeable and in a manner consistent with the training delivered by the United States Army. Many of his answers smacked of recent military training from army experts.

McDonald called his own boss and obtained permission to fly to Washington immediately and brief a trusted high-level colleague at the White House about the near disastrous domestic terrorism incident which if successful might have included some of President Trump's own family among the casualties.

CHAPTER 19 (White House Invitation)

After our celebratory breakfast on Sunday morning, we all showered and dressed.

My intention was to stay at the Skelding home tonight but then continue on my travel adventure tomorrow. Cindy was pregnant and I felt that my presence in their home was an imposition.

We were relaxing in the living-room in the early afternoon when the doorbell rang.

Donnie ran to answer it.

Standing in the doorway was a middle-aged gentleman in a military uniform and another very well-dressed chap.

Paul stood up to see what they wanted and then invited them inside.

"We're here to request the presence of Paul Skelding and Peter Montrose at the White House."

"What's this all about?" Paul inquired.

"It involves the incident at Trump Tower in New York City early on Saturday morning."

I stood up.

"I'm Peter Montrose. Am I under arrest?"

"You are not, sir. One of the occupants of the White House wants to thank you for your heroism."

"Why do they want to see me?" Paul inquired.

"I don't know sir but you were included in the invitation. Your wife and son are also welcome to accompany us if they'd like."

Both Cindy and Donnie jumped at the opportunity.

We followed the gentlemen to a couple of waiting SUV's. There was room for all four of us in the larger vehicle so we all climbed into that one.

Donnie was incredibly excited and so was I. I'd never even seen the White House and now it appeared that we might actually get to go inside.

We entered through one of the rear doors at which point Cindy, Paul and Donnie were offered a tour of the place. I was asked to accompany a middle-aged woman.

I was taken down an elevator and then led through some seriously fortified doors into an office area and from there into a conference room in which video equipment was set up.

Two older men entered and the lady who had escorted me left the room. They didn't introduce themselves.

"Are you Peter Montrose?" the one chap inquired.

"Yes I am."

"We've been informed that your expertise in bomb making saved a lot of folks from a horrible tragedy."

"I was thrilled that everything worked out well."

One of the men removed a lid from a sealed container to reveal what looked like a small helping of cheese and some crackers and other biscuits.

The smell was quite disgusting.

"Would you like some cheese and crackers?"

"I'm so sorry but my nose is extremely sensitive to aromas and the cheese is giving off an acrid odor. I think I'll pass on the snacks but thank you for offering them to me."

"Does the aroma remind you of anything?"

"I don't believe so. It's very sharp. Is that what they call Limburger cheese? I've heard of it but never tasted it or smelled it before now."

"Actually this is the explosive C-4. You're not really an explosives expert, are you Mr. Montrose?"

These bozos had tricked me. I might have known the invite was too good to be true.

"I must have a cold."

"It's also interesting that you don't remember me."

This was not good. I had no idea who the fellow was.

"I'm seventy-three and my eyesight is dreadful. Unless you were standing within two or three feet of me, I'd never be able to see your features clearly."

"I'm Colonel Ronald McDonald with Homeland Security. I interrogated you quite extensively in New York City immediately following the incident at Trump Tower. Your answers about explosives and bomb techniques were quite impressive then and I do believe that I've just confirmed why."

"I'm not following your reasoning."

"Let's bring in Paul Skelding and see if we can sort out the whole matter."

McDonald pulled out a smart phone and requested someone to bring Paul Skelding to Room 0016.

Five minutes of utter silence later, Paul was escorted into the room. The woman who brought him remained.

"This lady is Gloria Botting, one of the President's inner circle advisors."

Gloria spoke.

"Please be totally candid with us, Mr. Montrose and Mr. Skelding. It is imperative that we learn the truth about the recent events at Trump Tower."

I responded.

"You won't believe the truth. It's as simple as that."

"Run the recording of the phone call, Colonel," Gloria ordered.

For the next few minutes we listened to the entire conversation of the call from Bruhnsmon's apartment to Paul's home in the wee hours of Saturday morning.

"That call explains everything as clearly as we can make it," I admitted. "Paul and I had our bodies switched. In hindsight apparently the purpose of the switch was to allow my acute sense of smell to be married up to Paul's bomb defusing expertise in order to prevent the explosion.

Last night while we slept our bodies were switched back to normal."

"Can you prove that?" Gloria inquired.

"No. The only possible corroboration would come from Cindy, Donnie and Gerhard Bruhnsmon. I guess Paul and I can't prove that we weren't faking everything. You'll just have to take our word for it along with analyzing what few facts are available."

"What facts would those be?" Colonel McDonald asked.

"You could follow the phone calls. Paul and I never spoke on the telephone before his frantic phone call to Cindy on Thursday morning informing her that he had woken up in Syracuse in an old man's body. Paul and I never met in person until last evening when he returned to Washington in my body from New York City. All the investigation in the world can't disprove any of those statements."

"Believe me, we've been trying to link up the two of you at some point in the past but so far nothing indicates anything other than that the two of you were total strangers until Thursday. We've also found absolutely no previous connection between either of you and Gerhard Bruhnsmon, the security guard Blake Conrad, the bomber Grant Justin or the doorman who inadvertently triggered Mr. Justin's depraved act of revenge."

"Don't ask us to explain it," Paul Skelding interjected. "Peter and I were just unwitting pawns in some higher level game."

"I'm satisfied," Gloria asserted. "Peter and Paul, please follow me."

CHAPTER 20 (First Lady Appreciation)

Paul and I were escorted by Gloria up to the ground floor and taken to a very opulent room with lovely antique sofas and chairs.

A minute or so later, Cindy and Donnie were brought in to join us.

Donnie jabbered away about the neat stuff he had seen while the rest of us listened.

After about five minutes, First Lady Melania Trump entered the room.

Nobody was wearing a face mask.

Gloria introduced each of us to Mrs. Trump.

"Donald is in Texas at a political rally today and is unable to join us. The details of the attempted bombing of Trump Tower will be downplayed in the media to avoid any copycat ideas and of course the contents of the phone recording will be kept secret."

"It's always wise to prevent the public from being privy to unexplained phenomena such as this body switch episode," Gloria interjected. "Such revelations might induce panic. Please continue, Mrs. Trump."

"Thank you, Gloria. Our children have been informed of the bizarre but most welcome details about the purposeful switching of your bodies. Several of our immediate family members were in Trump Tower at the time of that divine intervention. America would have been devastated if the bomb had detonated as planned. Please accept my heartfelt gratitude and that of my entire family and the people of America for your crucial roles in preventing such a dreadful catastrophe."

Mrs. Trump walked up to each of us and hugged us.

We were escorted out of the room and taken to the SUV where we were driven back to Paul and Cindy's home.

Although Donnie was the most visibly ecstatic about our visit to the White House, we were all incredibly excited about the positive turn of events.

I decided to postpone my bus trip until Monday. It seemed prudent to stick around another day just in case the authorities needed to speak with us again.

As a celebratory treat, I had Indian food delivered to the house for our supper.

Our Sunday night sleep was uneventful and no further body switching took place.

CHAPTER 21 (An Eye-Opening Reward)

On Monday morning Paul received a call from the White House staffing office.

He was offered a job with security there and accepted the position without even needing to think about it.

It was both a promotion and the prospect of a much more useful and rewarding career.

Someone from the White House also phoned me later and asked if there was anything at all that the government could do for me as a reward for my service to America.

I made a joke that I didn't need anything unless they could improve my eyesight.

Imagine my surprise when they called back an hour later and indicated that a driver would arrive in ten minutes to take me to see a preeminent eye specialist.

That woman put me through a series of eye tests and immediately thereafter performed some laser surgery on my eyes right in her posh medical office.

She even had rooms in her office for surgical patients so that her staff could ensure that the patients recovered rapidly. I slept in one of her patient beds that night while my eyes were covered with surgical bandages.

On Tuesday afternoon the bandages came off and I could see distances clearly without even requiring eyeglasses.

The same woman who had set up this appointment with the eye doctor arrived to drive me back to Paul's house.

"I'm so grateful to your office. It's fantastic to be able to see again."

"Believe me, we are forever in your debt. Is there anything else we can do for you?"

"I hesitate to ask, but now that I can see, I'd like to drive again. My New York State license was yanked back in April of 2019 because of my eyesight. If I can get my license back, then I'll purchase a car and turn my permanent vacation into a driving holiday. It would be great to be able to say goodbye to smelly buses."

"What sort of automobile would best suit you?" the lady inquired.

"My last car which conked out in April of 2019 just a week before my license was yanked was a very basic 2002 Chevrolet Cavalier which I had purchased brand new way back in 2002. I hate the new vehicles because they're too complicated but I guess I won't have much choice. My ideal car would have as little computerized gadgetry as possible."

"That's interesting. We've arrived at Mr. Skelding's home. I may contact you later if I'm able to facilitate the reissuance of your New York State driver's license."

The Skeldings and I ordered in Chinese take-out food for our second successive celebratory supper.

The phone rang twice that evening.

The first call was President Trump himself calling to thank Paul and me for our service to America. The President even allowed Donnie and Cindy to get on the line for a moment. He was very patient and gracious. I gushed to President Trump about how I could now see like a young man and I thanked him for his office's role in making me whole again.

The second phone call brought another tremendous bit of news.

My New York State driver's license had been reinstated and a 2002 Chevrolet Cavalier in excellent shape and with low mileage had been duly transferred into my name.

Tomorrow a driver would arrive to deliver me to my new vehicle where I would also be provided with my driver's license.

I felt like an excited kid on Christmas morning.

On Wednesday morning I hugged Paul, Cindy and Donnie as we said our goodbyes. We vowed to stay in touch.

The driver arrived and took me to a vehicle compound.

CHAPTER 22 (On the Road Again)

My "new" 2002 Chevy was coincidentally the same black color as my own beloved and trusty vehicle had been.

My benefactors had provided me with road maps for every state in America.

Before I fired up my little beauty, I looked over the map of Virginia and noticed that the famous Blue Ridge Parkway began about eighty miles west of Washington.

I started up my vehicle and made my way to Interstate 66.

After about an hour I moved over to tiny Highway 55 which ran parallel to the Interstate.

At Front Royal I found a motel room.

Tomorrow morning I would begin my retirement journey at the extreme north end of the Blue Ridge Parkway and have a real travel adventure.

There would be no more stuffing myself onto stinky buses and being at the mercy of the bus routes and schedules while being forced to wear face masks constantly.

Peter Montrose was on the road again.

It was unlikely that the remainder of my journey would be as fascinating as the beginning of it had been.

On the drive today I decided to have a last will and testament prepared at an attorney's office somewhere on my trip and make Paul and Cindy my beneficiaries as well as my estate trustees. I had been remiss with my own legal affairs and had never bothered to write a new will after Deidre passed away in 1999.

That decision made me wonder if Donnie Skelding or the new baby would eventually select the law as their career. In any event, bequeathing Paul and Cindy my estate would provide the family with substantial financial security.

I pondered the extraordinary events of the past few days before I drifted off to sleep.

I was quite satisfied with the recent supernatural adventure.

Even though Paul Skelding had been the main player in the body switch saga, Peter Montrose's tired old body and acute sense of smell had also played a significant role in changing history for the better.

Despite a lengthy legal career in which I had made little impact on planet Earth, my role in the body switch adventure meant that Peter Montrose had helped to thwart evil in a major way.

It would undoubtedly be the biggest accomplishment of my mundane and lonely life.

THE END

ABOUT THE AUTHOR

Lance Majestik is a pen name of retired Canadian lawyer Donald W. Desaulniers who has written more than 100 novels under his real name or under his pen names Lance Majestik or Durward Garbage.

The books written under the names Lance Majestik or Durward Garbage tend to be shorter reads.

Desaulniers is a graduate of University of Waterloo (1968) and University of Western Ontario Law School (1971).

The author resides in Belleville, Ontario with his lovely British wife, Jane and their cat Charlie.

Please check out the Author Pages on Amazon for details about the novels written under the names Donald W. Desaulniers and Durward Garbage.

Listed below are the novels published under the pen name Lance Majestik:

OLD MIND, YOUNG BODY (Body Switch)

BETTER TIMES (A Comeback Story)

LOVE IN OLEAN (An American Romance)

UNDERCOVER TRUCKER (An American Mystery)

UNVACCINATED OLD LAWYER (Rebel Without a Jab)

CRAZY OLD LAWYER (A Talking Skin Tag)

LOVE MOCKS A LIMP DICK (War of the Sexes)

www.ingramcontent.com/pod-product-compliance
Lightning Source LLC
LaVergne TN
LVHW010949110826
845149LV00015B/3269
* 9 7 8 1 9 8 9 6 8 3 1 6 3 *